Magic Molly

The Good Luck Duck

D0315365

C555100866

Look out for more
Magic Molly books:

1. The Witch's Kitten
2. The Wish Puppy
3. The Invisible Bunny
4. The Secret Pony
5. The Shy Piglet

www.holly-webb.com

The girl who talks to animals

☆Magic Molly☆

The Good Luck Duck

HOLLY WEBB

Illustrated by Erica Jane Waters

■SCHOLASTIC

First published in the UK in 2012 by Scholastic Children's Books
An imprint of Scholastic Ltd
Euston House, 24 Eversholt Street
London, NW1 1DB, UK
Registered office: Westfield Road, Southam, Warwickshire, CV47 ORA
SCHOLASTIC and associated logos are trademarks
and/or registered trademarks of Scholastic Inc.

ISBN 978 1 407 13174 0

A CIP catalogue record for this book is available
from the British Library

Printed and bound by CPI Group (UK) Ltd, Croydon, CR0 4YY
Papers used by Scholastic Children's Books are made from
wood grown in sustainable forests.

1 3 5 7 9 10 8 6 4 2

www.scholastic.co.uk/zone
www.holly-webb.com

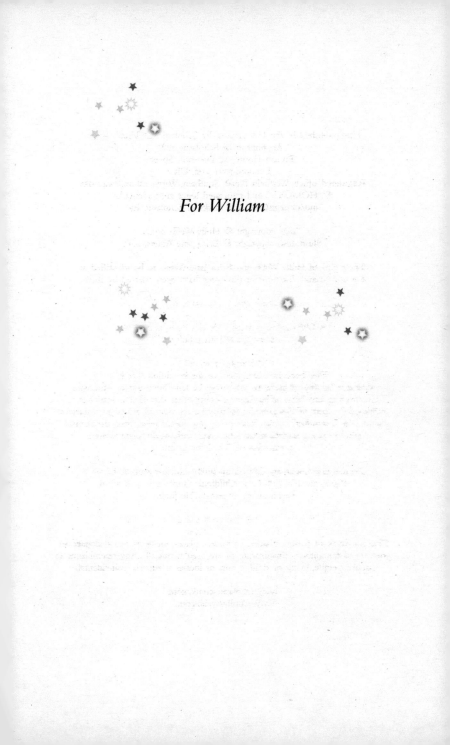

For William

Chapter One

Holiday Time!

"The holidays!" Molly shouted, dancing happily into the old farmhouse and flinging her school bag, lunch box, water bottle and PE kit into different corners of the kitchen. Then she went and picked them up again, before Mum could tell her to, but she was still dancing.

1

"Well, you're happy!" her dad laughed. "Would it be the holidays, by any chance?"

"Two whole weeks," Molly told him happily, sinking into a chair. "And it's sunny — almost like summer already. Do you need any help in the surgery this holiday, Dad?"

Her dad smiled. "Maybe. If I have any grumpy animals that need sweet-talking, I'll send for you."

Molly nodded. Her dad didn't know just how good at talking to animals she was. All the different pets that came to the surgery loved her, but every so often, Molly would find a really special one, a magical creature that could talk back.

A few weeks before, she had met a beautiful tabby kitten called Posy, who belonged to her little sister's friend

William from nursery. Molly had helped
Posy discover that she was a finding
kitten, and that her magic was for
searching out lost things. She'd stopped
the clever little kitten getting into all sorts
of trouble.

It would be so lucky if Molly could
meet another magical animal in the
holidays. She would have lots of time to
be at the surgery. Surely there must be

another magical creature out there who needed her help?

Molly got up to fetch some juice out of the fridge for herself and Kitty, her little sister. She could hear Mum and Kitty coming across the old farmyard to the house now, and Kitty was grumbling because Molly had run away too fast for Kitty to catch her.

She sighed to herself as she took the carton out of the fridge. Thinking about animals just made her wish that she could have a pet of her own. But Mum and Dad weren't keen on the idea. Dad always said that pets were a huge responsibility, and it would have to wait until they were older. That seemed a bit unfair to Molly, as it meant she couldn't have a pet until Kitty was old enough too.

Molly was almost sure, deep inside, that

she would be allowed a pet one day. A few months before, she had helped a pair of wish puppies, Star and Stella. They had granted Molly a wish, and she'd asked to have a pet of her own. It had to come true sooner or later.

Kitty charged into the kitchen and glared at Molly, who was still dreaming about her very own pet. "You ran off!"

Molly blinked. "Sorry. . . Juice?" She handed Kitty a cup, and Kitty eyed her grumpily for a minute, and then started to drink her juice.

"It's the holidays!" she said to their dad as soon as she'd downed the whole cupful. "It's Easter! There's chocolate!" Kitty went to nursery in the mornings, and the kitchen notice board was covered in her drawings of Easter chicks and eggs and rabbits. And an Easter penguin, which was probably meant to have been a chick, but Kitty had gone a bit haywire with a black crayon. She had been looking forward to Easter for ages.

Molly was too. She liked the chocolate eggs, obviously, but also there were loads of gorgeous baby lambs in the fields at the moment, and she loved going to look at them. Molly loved animals more than anything else.

She sipped her juice, listening to Kitty rattling on about the Easter bunny. That would be nice – an Easter bunny to talk to, perhaps with beautiful soft chocolate-coloured fur.

"Molly?"

Molly glanced up. Her mum was looking as though she'd asked something, but Molly had no idea what. "Sorry. . .?"

"Were you daydreaming about the holidays?" Her mum smiled. "I was saying that I saw a poster about a special Easter fun day at Marwell Hall on Saturday. There's an Easter Egg Hunt, arts and crafts, that sort of thing. I was wondering if we should go."

Molly nodded. "Yes, please. I love Marwell Hall." The big house close by was open to visitors, and often had special events on in the holidays. There was a huge lake in the ground, with loads of ducks, and Molly and Kitty loved to go and feed them.

"Can we ask Alice to come too?" Molly asked. Alice was her best friend from school.

Kitty looked up hopefully. "And William!"

Molly's mum nodded slowly. William could be quite a handful. "Perhaps William *and* his mum," she suggested, with a small sigh.

The Saturday they'd planned to go to Marwell House turned out to be beautifully sunny, so they decided to make a day of it and take a picnic.

"We should have a really special picnic," Molly pointed out. "It's the first picnic of the year."

"What would you like, to make it a really special picnic?" her mum asked.

"Um. Hard-boiled eggs. And everyone's favourite crisps. Lemonade. Oh, and chocolate Easter nests! You know, the kind you make with the cereal that looks like sticks."

"Have we got any?"

Molly burrowed into the cereal cupboard. "Yes, look, here's some!" she cried, pulling out the box.

"OK," said Mum. "And we can boil some eggs too. We're not going till later on this morning. You could put them in some food colouring and have special ones."

Molly nodded happily. This was turning into a proper Easter-y picnic. And then there would be the egg hunt afterwards too. Her dad had shown her in the local paper that there was a grand prize to win. Molly thought it might be an enormous chocolate egg!

Alice and Molly wandered down the lane, chatting. It was really nice seeing Alice out of school, Molly thought. They could have more fun, and chat as much as they liked without being told off by their teacher.

"This is William's house," she told Alice, and they stopped at the gate. "Oh, and look, there's his kitten! She's called Posy. She's really sweet. And so clever." Posy came running out as William's mum, Janey, opened the front door. She coiled herself lovingly around Molly's legs, rubbing her chin up and down Molly's socks.

Hello, Molly. It's been ages since I've seen you, Posy said, standing up on her hind paws and dabbing at Molly's knees until Molly picked her up. *You smell nice,* she said thoughtfully. *Very exciting, as though something special is going to happen today.*

What sort of something? Molly asked curiously, while she half-listened to Alice saying what a cute kitten Posy was. It was hard trying to talk to two people at the same time.

Maybe you're going to find something? Posy suggested. *That's usually what my magic is about, isn't it?*

Oh! We're going to an Easter Egg Hunt! Molly said delightedly. *Maybe I'm going to find the grand prize!*

Posy nosed at Molly's hair. *Maybe. . .*

Chapter Two

Hunting for Treasure

When they arrived at Marwell House, Molly, Alice and the others sat down by the lake in front of the big house to eat their picnic – but not too close. They had William with them, after all, and he would be in the lake trying to stroke the ducklings if he had half a chance. Actually, Molly would have liked to pet the ducklings as well – there were so many of them, yellow and brown and fluffy, so different to the crisp feathers of the big ducks. Their mothers were swimming round them, quacking anxiously and herding the babies in and out of the reeds.

Molly sat at the edge of the rug with Alice, nibbling her jam sandwiches, and then the boiled egg she'd dyed green with the food colouring. She turned round to eat that – it seemed rather mean to eat it in front of the ducks.

"These are so pretty," Alice said admiringly, holding up a pink egg. "I almost don't want to eat it, except I'm starving."

"Can we eat the nests now?" Kitty asked for about the fifth time, burrowing eagerly into the picnic bag.

The mums laughed and shared them out, each one topped with three little chocolate eggs. "Don't take too long eating them," Molly's mum said. "The treasure hunt starts at two, and it's half past one already. We need to go down past the house to the wood."

Molly and the others ate the nests quickly – they could already see lots of other families heading through the gardens to the wood, and they didn't want to miss the start of the hunt.

The ducks were creeping out of the reeds now, peering curiously at the crumbs left from so many picnics. A fat brown duck with a line of seven little ducklings behind her hurried past, snapping up sandwich crusts, and Kitty reached for a fluffy brown duckling to stroke, but it scuttled out of her way, cheeping crossly.

"I only wanted to stroke it," Kitty said sadly.

"Never mind," Molly told her. "Let's go and do the treasure hunt." She pulled her little sister up, and they folded the picnic rug, tucking it away in their mum's bag. Alice took out the four little baskets she'd brought from home, for collecting the chocolate eggs in, and handed them around. Kitty and William raced ahead through the gardens with their baskets, calling excitedly to each other about chocolate eggs.

Molly looked back at the lake for one last sight of the ducklings, but this time it wasn't the furry little bundles pecking at crumbs that caught her eye.

A white duck was hurrying along the edge of the lake, nosing among the water plants, pattering this way and that. It was hard to tell – Molly didn't know that much about ducks – but she looked as though she had lost something. There was a definite worry about her waddle, her head was darting back and forth and she was making anxious little quacking noises.

Molly took a step towards her, but then her mum called, "Molly! Come on! We'll be late!"

The white duck's wings flapped out in surprise, and she darted away into the water, frightened by the loud noise.

Molly sighed. "Sorry!" she murmured. "I hope you find whatever it is you've lost. And I do hope it isn't your babies," she added, with a worried frown. There were so many ducklings around, and they all looked alike to her, although probably not to the mother ducks.

She raced off after the others, and they arrived at the wood where the hunt had been laid out. There were lots of people there to take part, and the organizers were hurrying around looking rather worried. Molly heard a couple of girls in Marwell House shirts saying that they needed more eggs, right now, and one of them went dashing off. The other one went into the wood with a basket of golden eggs, and everyone in the line chattered excitedly as they saw her stooping and hiding one of the eggs somewhere in a hollow below the trees.

"Those look *yummy*," Kitty sighed.

"I think they've got more people here than they were expecting," Janey, William's mum, said. "It's probably because of the nice weather."

Now the staff were walking down the line, explaining how the egg hunt would work. "You need to follow the rabbits," the girl standing by Molly, Kitty, Alice and William explained. "There are lots of little golden eggs around, but if you follow the rabbits, they'll point you in the direction of the grand prize. So when the whistle blows, look for the rabbits, OK?"

They nodded excitedly, and Molly wondered for a moment if they would be real rabbits. But she thought probably not. Rabbits weren't very good at staying still, and she couldn't imagine how they'd be much use as clues.

"There's the whistle!" Alice squeaked, and they surged forward, a line of excited children racing into the wood. There were so many that Molly lost Alice and the others in the first couple of minutes. She glanced around worriedly, and saw her mother waving.

"Don't worry, Molly! We'll find you at

the end! Just stay by the entrance to the wood. I've told Alice too."

Molly nodded, but she wished she knew where Alice was. It would be more fun to do the hunt together. Still, there was no point just standing there. She started to look around for the little golden eggs, and the rabbits too. Then she laughed out loud – there was a toy rabbit in the tree above her head, tied into position so that he was pointing his furry paw along the path.

Molly hurried along in the direction he was showing, and spotted a glint of gold in the fork between two tree branches. She picked up the egg, feeling pleased with herself, and went on, scanning the branches above her head for rabbits. But the next one was at her feet, standing in a hole at the bottom of a tree, as though he was coming out of his burrow. He was pointing along the same path. Molly could hear other people blundering about in the wood, calling to each other, but no one seemed to have seen this rabbit.

"Oh!" she said happily, seeing another golden egg hidden in some bracken. This one had a ribbon round it, a red one. Perhaps it was a prize egg!

She was just reaching out to pick it up when someone crashed through the bracken and grabbed it first.

"Hey!" Molly cried. "I saw that one!"

"So what?" The red-haired girl clutched the egg close and glared at Molly. "You didn't pick it up, did you? I got it first, that's what matters."

"Yeah!" snapped another girl, who was a little smaller, with the same red hair.

They had to be sisters. "You're just too slow." The two girls sniggered together and rustled off through the bracken, leaving Molly staring after them. The egg was a really big one. It was sure to be a special prize, she thought crossly, slumping down on a fallen tree and looking gloomily at her two little golden eggs. She wished she hadn't lost Alice. The egg hunt was no fun all alone. She sighed, and wondered if eating one of the eggs would cheer her up. Posy had been wrong – it wasn't a day for Molly to find things at all.

She was just starting to unwrap the golden foil when there was a rustling noise in the bracken. Molly looked up sharply, wondering if it was those horrible girls coming back. But instead, a snow-white duck hurried out of the green leaves, her crisp white feathers shining with a greenish-golden glow in the dappled sunlight of the wood.

The duck was very pretty, but she still looked worried — it was the same duck from the lake, Molly realized as she watched the white creature hurry along the path.

It was the same duck, and she was *talking*. . .

Chapter Three

The Lost Egg

"Wherever has he got to? Oh, where can he be?" the duck muttered anxiously.

"Hello!" Molly called quietly, not wanting to frighten the white duck.

The duck twisted her long neck around and peered worriedly at Molly. "Have you seen an egg?" she asked. She didn't seem to be very surprised that Molly was talking to her.

"Ummm . . . like these?" Molly held out the two gold-foiled eggs she'd found.

"No, of course not! A proper egg! My egg!" the duck wailed.

"Oh!" Molly shook her head. "No, I'm really sorry, I haven't. But I'll help you look, if you like. When did you last see it?"

"This morning," the duck muttered, her head turning this way and that as she gazed unhappily around. "I can't think where it's gone."

"Did you go off to find some food?" Molly asked. She wasn't quite sure how sitting on eggs worked. Did ducks have to stay with them all the time? It would be terribly boring, she thought.

The duck sighed sadly. "Yes. I was so hungry, and there were some delicious beetles wandering past." She stared at Molly sideways with one dark, sparkly eye. "And then I couldn't help going for a little walk. I tucked my egg up very safely under the geranium leaves in the flower bed in front of the house. The buds are showing on those geraniums, you know. They'll be pink ones, I think. Very bright, cheerful flowers. I thought he'd like them."

Molly nodded. "Is he due to hatch soon?"

The duck sighed again. "I do hope so. He's taking an awfully long time. But I simply couldn't stay sitting on my nest any more. I had to go for a little walk."

"It must be very hard, hatching eggs," Molly agreed.

"Oh, you wouldn't believe how hard," the duck nodded. "Sitting still in one place for weeks and weeks! And nothing to look at. Just reeds, and reeds, and reeds." She eyed Molly again. "Reeds are really not very exciting," she explained. Then she gave a panicky little flap of her wings. "My egg! I almost forgot!" And she hurried off, waddling anxiously this way and that across the path. "I can't think what can have happened to it. Why would anybody want to move my egg? And I can't believe it was a fox. There are just too many people about, I don't know why."

"Oh, it's because of the Easter Egg Hunt," Molly explained.

The duck looked up at her. "Eggs. . .?" she asked faintly.

Molly nodded slowly. "Yeees, but chocolate ones. No one would mistake your egg for a chocolate one, would they? Won't it be brown, like a hen's egg?"

"Certainly not!" the duck said huffily. "Usually my eggs would be a beautiful pure blue-white. But this one is special. It's a much deeper blue. Almost sky blue." She stared at Molly in horror. "Do you think someone might mistake it for one of the eggs from the hunt?" she asked.

"I've got a horrible feeling they might have done," Molly admitted. "The people organizing it were rushing around everywhere; I think they didn't have enough eggs for the number of people who arrived. If one of them saw a pretty egg in the flower bed, they might just think it had been dropped there by accident, and then they'd add it to the eggs for the trail, wouldn't they?"

"My egg!" the duck wailed. "What if someone tries to eat it? And there are so

many people." The duck fluttered her wings worriedly. "Rushing about all over the place, and any one of them could so easily step on my egg. Or drop it! Oh dear!"

Molly nodded worriedly. "We'd better hurry up and find it. But don't worry, I've found two eggs already," Molly told her. "I'm sure we can find yours. What's your name?" She felt silly just thinking of her as the duck.

"Lucy," the duck told her. "And when he hatches, my egg will be called Herbert. I think. Or perhaps John? Oh, I don't know! I can't believe this has happened, I really can't."

Molly nodded. "It's ever such bad luck," she said sympathetically.

The duck stared at her. "But that's just it! It shouldn't be. I'm a good luck duck, you see. And my egg will be too. In fact, I think he might the luckiest duck I've ever seen, he has such a beautiful big blue shell. We really shouldn't be having bad luck at all!"

Chapter Four

Lucy's Luck

"A good luck duck?" Molly said slowly. "I've never heard of one of those."

"Well, we're ever so rare," Lucy told her proudly. "And extremely special."

"Do you really give people good luck?"

"Of course. Which is why it's so very strange that I should lose my egg!" Lucy set off down the path again, calling anxiously. "Egg! Egg! Herbert! Jonty! Whatever your name is! Oh, do come back!"

"It can't," Molly pointed out, and the duck stared at her as though she'd said something mad. "I mean, eggs can't move, can they?"

"Oh." The duck concentrated hard, her eyes almost bulging. "No. I suppose not. But he can definitely hear me from inside his shell. I don't want him to think I'm not looking for him!" She darted into the bracken as a couple of boys ran past, one of them already smeared in chocolate up to his ears. "Look! They're *eating* them!

Oh, egg, where have you gone?"

Molly followed her down the path,
lifting the bracken every so often to see if
there was an egg hidden underneath. "So
it's a blue egg?" she asked.

"A beautiful, beautiful blue," the duck
agreed. "Sky blue. With a hint of green.
And silver."

"Oh." Molly nodded. She was finding it
hard to imagine. "And how big?"

"Very big. Much, much bigger than
any of the other ducks' eggs," she added
proudly.

Molly sighed quietly. That wasn't
particularly helpful. Still, she was sure
most of the eggs from the hunt were
golden, so a blue one ought to be
obvious. If only they had some idea
where it had been hidden. It could be
anywhere in the wood.

I wish Posy had come with us, Molly thought worriedly. Then Molly's eyes widened. *Oh!* Maybe Posy hadn't meant that she would find the prize egg in the hunt at all – perhaps she had been talking about Lucy's egg instead!

Suddenly Molly felt a lot more hopeful. She was certain Posy wouldn't have got it wrong. They were bound to find the egg now. They just needed a bit of luck, to  make sure no one else found it first. Molly frowned, and then looked hopefully at Lucy.

"Lucy, couldn't you do a good luck spell? So that we find your egg before anyone else does."

Lucy stopped waddling down the path and stared up at her. "Why didn't I think of that?" she muttered. "Oh, I don't know whether I'm on my beak or my tail, I really don't. A spell, of course. . ." She closed her eyes and spread out her wings – the beautiful crisp white feathers shimmering and sparkling in the dim light of the wood.

Molly drew in a delighted breath as silvery points of light began to dance up and down Lucy's feathers, so that she glowed all over.

"Luck. . ." Lucy whispered. "Luck for a good luck duck – stuck in the muck. . . Oh, that's no good." The silvery shimmer over her feathers faded a little. "This is so difficult. I'm so worried, I just can't think properly!"

"Ssshhh!" Molly put a finger to her lips. "I think someone else is coming." She could hear voices, cross voices. People arguing, it sounded like, and coming their way.

"We're never going to find the grand prize, Sarah!" someone moaned. "Can't we stop now? I'm bored. And we've got lots of little ones. I want to sit down and eat some of them."

Molly saw Lucy shudder at the thought.

"Katy, shut up!" This voice sounded older but equally fed up. "I'm not stopping. We've been all through this stupid wood. It has to be here somewhere. I won't go home without it, so there!"

"Well, I want to go home noooowww!" wailed the younger voice, and Molly suddenly realized as they came round the twist in the path – it was the horrible red-haired girls who'd snatched the other egg from her before. She was glad they hadn't found the grand prize. They didn't deserve it.

"You again!" snapped the older sister, Sarah.

Molly glared at her, and Lucy shrank back behind a tree, not wanting the girls to see her.

"If the grand prize was here, *she'd* have found it," Sarah said nastily to Katy. "Come on, let's go and look further along the path." They ran off, giggling meanly and making faces at Molly.

Lucy poked her head out from behind the tree, staring after them in horror. "I hope they don't find my egg! They were horrible!"

"They really were," Molly agreed. "But I bet they won't find it. Not unless someone else shows them it first. Lucy, do you think the spell worked at all? Did we get some luck?"

Lucy sighed. "I'm not sure. I didn't quite finish it."

"You went very shiny and beautiful," Molly told her. "You looked as though you were doing amazing magic."

"Really?" Lucy ducked her head shyly, and Molly was sure there was a faint pink tinge to her feathers all of a sudden. "Well, maybe it worked a little. But it wasn't a full luck spell, I'm afraid."

"Never mind." Molly stroked Lucy's

smooth head gently. "Try calling the egg again," she suggested. "Would he be able to answer you?"

"Yes. He's talking already," Lucy said proudly. "Only a little, of course. Just a few words."

"Well, at least we'll know if we get close, then," Molly said, feeling relieved. It would have been awful if they'd walked straight past the egg without ever knowing he was there.

"Egg! Dear egg! Where are you?" Lucy called again and again as they wandered along the paths, her voice growing more whispery and anxious every time.

At last she sat down, tucking her smooth white head under one wing. "Perhaps we'll never find him," she said quietly to Molly, her voice feather-muffled, so that Molly had to lean close to hear. "Or maybe someone else has found him already!"

Molly sighed and sat down on a tree stump. "I suppose they might have done," she admitted.

"I'm cold. . ."

Molly nodded. "Me too, a bit. It's probably because we're sitting still." She took a breath. "We should get up and keep looking." She didn't jump up, though, and neither did Lucy. Both of them felt rather hopeless.

"Ever so cold. . ." the little voice whispered again, and Molly blinked.

"Was that you?" she asked the duck.

Lucy pulled her head from under her wing. "I thought it was you!"

"I'm so cold!" It was more of a wail this time, a quiet little moan, and Molly jumped to her feet, looking this way and that.

"What's that?" she squeaked. "Did you hear it?"

"It's my egg!" Lucy was dancing around the path, fluttering her wings excitedly. "He's near! He's close! I'm coming to find you, egg!"

She darted up the path, zigzagging between the bracken clumps and calling for her baby. Molly raced after her, listening for the tiny voice.

"He's here! Look!" Lucy flapped to a halt behind a tree, and opened her wings lovingly.

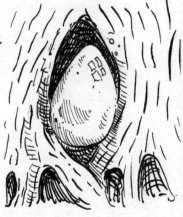

"Oh! We found it!" Molly gasped. Hidden in a hollow twisted from two fat old roots, was a beautiful, shining blue egg. "It's just as lovely as you said it was," she told Lucy, and the white duck preened happily. "Isn't it?" she whispered. "The spell must have worked."

But Molly was staring anxiously down the path. "I don't think it gave us quite enough luck. I can hear those girls coming back!"

Lucy gave a squeaky quack of horror. "They mustn't have my egg! Hide it, Molly!"

"What have you found?" Sarah and Katy were running back towards them. "We heard you saying you'd found something! Have you found the grand prize? That isn't fair! We're going to find it! Give it here!"

"No!" Molly yelped, leaning over the egg and trying to shield it with her hands. She didn't want to pick it up – eggs were so fragile, and it would be so awful if she broke it.

"Let me see!" Sarah reached out to push her away, and suddenly there was

a flurry of white feathers and furious quacking, and Lucy was there, protecting Molly and her egg.

"What's that flapping thing?" Katy squealed, and Sarah jumped back with a yelp as Lucy nipped at her sandals.

"Run, Molly! Pick the egg up and run!" Lucy hissed.

Chapter Five

Magic Hatching

Molly raced through the wood, twisting and turning from path to path, ducking under branches and scrambling through brambles. She wasn't giving up *this* egg to those two. She was sure that Sarah and Katy would try to chase her once they'd got over their fright and realized that Lucy was just a duck, and not some horrible monster.

There was a scuffling noise behind her, and Molly glanced round anxiously,

wondering if they'd caught her up
already.

But it was Lucy, half running, half
flying after her. "I frightened them off! I
think they thought I was a swan!" Then
she quacked delightedly. "We found him!
We found him!" she squawked. "Ooh,
Molly, slow down!"

"Sorry!" Molly stopped, and leaned
against a tree, panting. "You're sure they've
gone? I just don't want them to catch us."

"No, quite right,"
Lucy said seriously. "I
dread to think what
they would have done
with my poor little
egg."

Molly looked
around. They were
in a quiet, dark little

tangle of trees. It felt as though they were right in the middle of the wood. The new leaves fluttered gently on the trees, but there wasn't another sound. "It feels like we've come far away from everyone else on the Easter Egg Hunt," she told Lucy. "We can stop for a bit, I think. I'm all out of breath too." She sat down on a big sticking-out tree root and laid the egg in her lap, gazing at it admiringly. "It's really beautiful, Lucy."

"I know," the white duck said proudly, hopping up on to the root next to her.

The egg was a deep greenish-blue, but it shimmered all over, like the really lovely sort of glitter in Molly's best art set. Only better. Molly stroked it, very gently, and it started to glow. "Oh, Lucy, look. . ." Molly murmured. "It wasn't doing that before."

Lucy leaned her smooth head up

against the egg and then looked up at Molly, her eyes sparkling. "It's going to hatch soon, I'm sure of it. Very, very soon! We've found it just in time. Imagine what would have happened if someone else had found it, and he hatched! I might never have seen him again."

They both stared at the egg in Molly's lap. It was really glittering now, the little crystal speckles in the shell glowing and dimming and glowing again, so that shining waves of light ran over it.

Lucy nuzzled it lovingly again. "Look at all that magic! Such a special egg! I told you, Molly, didn't I? This is going to be such a lucky duckling. Doing magic like that, even in

50

the egg! I've never seen anything like it."

"Oh look!" Molly breathed. "A crack, can you see?"

A tiny golden crack ran round the middle of the shell. Molly could see it slowly creeping along. A soft light shone out of it, as though there was a candle burning inside the egg.

"Your baby's glowing," she whispered to Lucy.

Lucy nodded proudly. "Come along, egg dearest," she whispered, and the egg suddenly split in two, leaving a small golden duckling sitting inside. He stared up at them shyly, and then sneezed and shook himself all over.

"He's beautiful," Molly said quietly, as Lucy gently nudged her baby, and he nuzzled up against her.

Lucy nodded. "Of course he is," she said proudly. "But without you, Molly, I might never have found him in time. We need to thank you properly."

Molly stared at her. "What do you mean?"

Lucy opened out her white wings, and the feathers sparkled gently in the faint sunlight. Molly would have loved to stroke them, but she wasn't sure if ducks really enjoyed being stroked.

She blinked in surprise as Lucy stroked her instead, fluttering the crisp feathers down Molly's cheek. They were warm, and they tingled over Molly's skin. She could feel the magic in the feathers as it bubbled through her, and she laughed out

loud. "I'm sparkling," she told Lucy. "So
are you, and so's your duckling."

He was, little shimmers of gold running
over his fluffy down feathers. He squeaked
excitedly and shook himself, almost falling
over backwards as he tried to see all over

himself and watch the sparkly luck magic.

Molly sighed blissfully. "Was that the good luck magic that you gave me just then? I do feel lucky, all of a sudden."

"Of course," Lucy nodded. "I feel so much better now, I could do any amount of magic. But you'd better use it up quickly, Molly. It's been a busy day, and I'm not sure how long the magic will last."

Molly nodded. "We need to go back into the busier part of the wood, because I'm sure I can find lots of eggs now. Maybe even the grand prize." She stretched out her fingers in front of her and giggled. "Look, I'm still glittering. Maybe everyone will just think it's glitter hairspray or something."

Lucy eyed Molly thoughtfully, as she hurried the duckling along beside her. "I think it won't show once we're out in the sunshine. Which is a pity, because it looks very nice." She looked at Molly with her head on one side for a minute, and added, "For someone without feathers," in a pitying sort of voice.

Molly tried not to laugh. She didn't mind Lucy being rude – she obviously didn't mean to be, she just really did think that feathers were nicest. "I can hear Kitty! That's my sister," she added in a whisper, as the path through the wood seemed to open up almost magically, leading her straight to Kitty and Alice, crouching beside a clump of bracken. "Wow! Your good luck magic works brilliantly. We found them straight away!"

"Of course," Lucy told her. "Now get looking for that grand prize!"

"Is that fair, though?" Molly whispered

back. "If I've got all the good luck –
maybe I shouldn't. . ."

"Don't be silly!" Lucy hissed. "We gave
it to you because you helped us! You
did something nice, and now something
nice will happen to you. It's perfectly fair.
Besides, this is my house and my lake and
my wood. If I say you should win, you
should!"

Molly grinned at her. "I suppose so."

Lucy shooed her duckling gently into
the ferns and wafted a wing at Molly.

"Go! We need to get back to the lake. I need to show him the water. If he doesn't get to like it straight away, he might never want to swim. We'll see you later, Molly, when you've found that grand prize."

Chapter Six

The Clever Clue

Molly watched Lucy and the duckling disappear among the leaves, just a flash of white tail bobbing away, with a little sunny yellow patch of fluff following after. Then she turned, smiling. "Hello, Alice! Hey, Kitty!"

"Molly!" Alice ran towards her delightedly. "We lost you ages ago. Your mum's looking for you too."

"And William ran off! Have you got chocolate?" Kitty demanded.

"A couple of the little eggs, that's all,"
Molly told her. "How about you two?"

Kitty showed her the little pink basket
Alice had brought for her, which was
almost full of eggs.

"I'm very good at finding them," she
said happily. "But Mum says I can't have
any more!" she added grumpily. "And I'm
not allowed to eat all of these today in
case I'm sick."

"Never mind. You can help me and Alice look," Molly told her. "I'm suddenly feeling very lucky. I think we should go and look for the grand prize."

Alice looked at her excitedly. "Oooh, have you found a clue to where it is?"

"Um, sort of. . ." Molly nodded, knowing that she couldn't really explain all her sudden good luck. "Anyway, I think the grand prize is. . ." She closed her eyes for a moment, and twirled slowly on the spot, watching the sparkly patterns behind her eyelids. Suddenly there was a rush of silvery glitter, and she stopped. "That way!" she said, opening her eyes and pointing down a very faint path through the bracken. It looked as though it was only used by rabbits.

"Really?" Alice asked doubtfully.

"Really." Molly nodded. She was sure the magic was leading her that way. Kitty ran ahead of them on to the path and squeaked with delight. "Look, another rabbit! It must be the right way!"

The rabbit was perched in a hole in one of the trees, and his brown fur was so soft and silky that he almost looked real. There was a little sign hanging around his neck, which said, *The grand prize is hiding with King Charles.*

"What does that mean?" Alice asked blankly.

61

Kitty looked from Molly to Alice, her eyes hopeful. She had no idea either, and she was expecting the big girls to solve the clue, Molly realized.

"King Charles," she muttered. "We've never done anything about him in school, but I've heard about him somewhere, I know I have. . ."

"He was the king who had to run away, I think." Alice sounded doubtful.

"Yes!" Molly hugged her. "That's it, Alice! He had to escape after his army was defeated in a battle, Grandad told me about it. And he had to hide from the other army; they had soldiers out looking for him."

"Where?" Alice gasped. "Where did he hide?"

"In an oak tree!" Molly whispered to them both. "So we just have to find one. It'll probably be quite big, if it's got a

place in it to hide a special
prize. Oak trees are the ones
with the wavy edges on the
leaves, Kitty."

Kitty nodded, frowning.
"Like those ones over there?"

Molly looked round
hopefully to see where her
little sister was pointing.
"Yes! You star, Kitty."

They ran over to the big
tree, which was spreading
its branches over a little
clearing in the wood.

63

"It's huge," Molly murmured. The oak had a thick trunk, but it was the branches that were so amazing. They curled and twisted almost down to the ground in some places, making strange, beautiful shapes.

"Can we climb it?" Kitty asked hopefully. She didn't wait for an answer, running over to the nearest branch and pulling herself up. "Oh, it's nice! It's easy to climb!"

"Be careful," Molly told her, a little anxiously – but at least Kitty wasn't very high up. She went closer, stroking the pitted bark. It was so rough that it almost looked striped.

Alice walked all round the tree trunk and came back shaking her head. "I can't see any holes."

"It must be balanced in the branches,"

Molly decided. "Can you see anything, Kitty?"

"No," Kitty said crossly. "Only a stupid picture of an egg. I don't want a picture, I want a chocolate one!"

"Kitty!" Molly and Alice yelled together. "Please can you get it?" Molly added nicely. "It's probably another clue."

"Oh, all right," Kitty muttered, and handed her a large cardboard egg, painted pink with yellow spots. PRIZE was written across it, in big blue letters.

Molly took it, turning it over excitedly. "Oh, wow! It says the real grand prize egg is too big to hide up a tree! We have to take this to the tent at the entrance to the wood, and they'll give us the real one."

Just then they heard a bell ringing in the distance. "That's for the end of the hunt," Alice said. "We found the egg just in time."

Molly smiled. "That was lucky, wasn't it?"

Molly, Alice and Kitty hurried to the gate at the end of the wood, eager to claim the grand prize egg.

"We should all share it," Molly said as they came out into the gardens and saw the tent. "Alice, you helped me solve the clue, and Kitty found the actual egg. So I think we found it together."

She handed the cardboard egg to the lady sitting behind the table, looking at her hopefully.

"You found it! Oh, well done, we were beginning to think no one had solved the clue." She beamed at them and reached

under the white tablecloth, pulling out a
wicker basket, in which was the biggest
chocolate egg that Molly had ever seen.
It was milk chocolate, but decorated with
swirls of white and dark chocolate too, so
that it had a beautiful marbly pattern all
over it.

Molly couldn't help licking her lips, and Kitty looked as though she was going to explode with excitement. "It's bigger than my head!" she squeaked.

"They won it! It's that girl. . ." someone hissed furiously behind them, and Molly looked round to see the red-haired sisters staring at them in disgust.

She didn't say anything. She didn't need to. If they hadn't been so mean and snatched that first egg off her, she might never have met Lucy. She just smiled. "Molly! There you all are!" Mum came over to them looking relieved, with Janey and William, who was covered in chocolate.

"We won, Mum!" Molly showed her the egg – it was very heavy.

"Oh my goodness. . . Well, that might last you a couple of days," Mum said faintly.

"We all found it together, so we're sharing it," Molly told her.

"It looks gorgeous," her mum said, hugging her. "Well done."

"Can we go to the playground?" Kitty asked hopefully, as they walked past it on the way back to the footpath. There was a little playground close to the gates of Marwell House.

"Yes, let's, Mum," Molly agreed. She didn't really feel like going on swings or anything like that – she was worn out from all the racing around in the wood. But she didn't want to go home just yet. She was hoping to see Lucy and the duckling again before they went, and the playground wasn't all that far from the lake.

When they got the playground, Kitty and William begged Alice to push them on the swings. The two mums were chatting, so Molly nipped quietly over to the bushes on the lake side of the playground. She could just see the glint of water over round the side of Marwell House.

"Molly!"

Molly jumped. "Lucy, you're here!"

A white head was peering carefully out of the bushes, and Molly crouched down behind a clump of rose bushes to talk to her, smiling at the little golden duckling, who was peeping at her round his mother's tail.

"I'm so glad to see you. I didn't want to go without saying goodbye."

Lucy nodded. "I'm sorry I had to hurry off before. It was important for Henry to see the lake. It isn't right for ducklings to be too far away from water, you know."

Molly laughed. "Henry?" It was such
a big, grown-up sounding name. It
didn't make her think of a little fluffy
duckling at all. She looked at him again
thoughtfully, and he stared back with
those sparkling black eyes. Now she
thought about it, she could imagine him
growing up into a plump, serious-looking
white duck. *Then* he would be a Henry.

"Did it work? Did you find the grand
prize?" Lucy asked eagerly.

"Yes! And it's huge, Lucy, the biggest chocolate egg I've ever seen. But not nearly as beautiful as Henry's egg," Molly added quickly. "The spell was brilliant."

"Good. That was your first spell, dearest," Lucy told the duckling, nudging him gently with her beak. "You deserved it, Molly."

"Molly!" It was Alice calling her. They must be wondering where she was.

"I have to go," she told Lucy reluctantly. "But I'll come back and see you soon," she promised. "We come to Marwell House lots. I'll bring you some tuna sandwiches! You'll love those."

Lucy nuzzled against Molly's cheek, and Molly felt that glorious glittery good-luck feeling again. "We'll watch out for you," she promised, setting out across the playground to the lake with Henry close behind her. He looked back as they reached the gate, and flicked the little stub of his tail at her cheekily.

"Goodbye, Molly! Good luck!"

HOLLY has always loved animals. As a child, she had two dogs, a cat, and at one point, nine gerbils (an accident). Holly's other love is books. Holly now lives in Reading with her husband, three sons and a very spoilt cat.

5 Quick Questions for Holly Webb

1. Kittens or puppies? Kittens

2. Chocolate or Sweets? Chocolate

3. Favourite websites? Lolcats

4. Favourite colour? Green

5. Favourite film? The Sound of Music

Read more about Molly's
magical adventures!

The girl who talks to animals

Magic Molly

The Witch's Kitten

HOLLY WEBB

Molly has a
magical way with animals!

Sparkle the kitten is lost and he needs Molly's help to get back home.

But that means going into the spooky wood . . . and to the witch's cottage!

The girl who talks to animals

Magic Molly

The Wish Puppy

HOLLY WEBB

Molly has a
magical way with animals!

**No one knows why Star, the
King Charles Spaniel, is so unhappy.**

**Will Molly be able to help before
Star's magic disappears for ever?**

The girl who talks to animals

Magic Molly

The Invisible Bunny

HOLLY WEBB

Molly has a
magical way with animals!

Snowdrop the rabbit is behaving very oddly. Not only does she have the hiccups – she keeps disappearing!

Will Molly be able to find her before her owner returns?

The girl who talks to animals

☆ -Magic Molly- ☆

The Secret Pony

HOLLY WEBB

Molly has a
magical way with animals!

Silver the pony has a very special secret. He's really a unicorn and more than anything he wants to be free.

Can Molly find somewhere he will be happy?

The girl who talks to animals

Magic Molly

The Shy Piglet

HOLLY WEBB

Molly has a magical way with animals!

When Molly meets a piglet at the local farm, she can't believe he is scared to play with others.

Can Molly help him overcome his shyness?